If I Lived In Germany . . .

Published by
LONGSTREET PRESS, INC.
A subsidiary of Cox Newspapers,
A subsidiary of Cox Enterprises, Inc.
2140 Newmarket Parkway
Suite 118
Marietta, GA 30067

Printed in the United States of America

1st printing 1995

Library of Congress Catalog Card Number: 95-77256

ISBN 1-56352-235-7

This book was printed by Horowitz/Rae, Fairfield, NJ
Electronic film prep and separations by Advertising Technologies, Inc., Atlanta, GA

Jacket design by Neil Hollingsworth
Book Design by Jill Dible

Special thanks to Christa Babel, Joan Brandt, Diane Dear, Barbara Hager, Roswitha Langer, Annette Witte and the Goethe-Institut Atlanta for their helping us insure the accuracy of our use of the German language and our depiction of cultural details.

If I Lived
In Germany . . .

By Rosanne Knorr
Illustrated by John Knorr

LONGSTREET PRESS, INC.
Atlanta, Georgia

Also by Rosanne and John Knorr

If I Lived In France…
If I Lived In Spain…
If I Lived In Japan…

German customs and words
Are quite easy, you'll see.
Just visit *Deutschland*
And pretend to be me!

If I lived in Germany,
My bright, happy voice
Would let everyone know,
"Ich spreche Deutsch."

German word:	**Sounds like. . .**	**And it means. . .**
Ich spreche Deutsch	eek SHPREK-uh doytch	I speak German
Mein Name ist...	mine NAH-muh ist	My name is...

When I greet all my friends
Who live down the block,
I don't say, "Hello" —
I say, *"Guten Tag."*

German word:	Sounds like. . .	And it means. . .
Guten Tag	GOO-ten tahk	Good day

I ask with a smile,
"Wie geht's?" "How are you?"
My friend will then say,
"Mir geht's gut," — "I'm OK."

I give a small wave —
The meaning is plain.
I'm saying "Goodbye."
That's *"Auf Wiedersehen!"*

German word:	Sounds like. . .	And it means. . .
Mir geht's gut	meer gayts goot	I'm okay
Wie geht's?	vee gayts	How are you?
Auf Wiedersehen!	owf VEE-der-zane	Goodbye

My day begins early.
I rise from *mein Bett*
And head for *die Küche*,
Where breakfast is set.

German word:	Sounds like. . .	And it means. . .
mein Bett	mine bet	my bed
die Küche	dee koo-chuh	the kitchen
mein Frühstück	mine FROO-schtook	my breakfast
das Brot	dahs broht	bread

I start off my day
With good things to eat.
Mein Frühstück includes
Brot, *Käse* and meat.

German word:	Sounds like. . .	And it means. . .
der Honig	dayr HOH-nig	honey
der Käse	dayr kay-suh	cheese
der Orangensaft	dayr oh-RANZ-en-zahft	orange juice
die Milch	dee meelch	milk

When I greet *meine Mutter*,
I say, *"Guten Morgen."*
Then *mein Vater* walks in,
So I say it again.

German word:	Sounds like. . .	And it means. . .
meine Mutter	my-nuh MOO-ter	mother
Guten Morgen	GOO-ten MORE-gen	good morning
mein Vater	mine FAH-ter	father
Vati	FAH-tee	papa
Mutti	MOO-tee	mommy

My school day is short.
It lasts eight to one.
But some weeks it's *Samstag*
Before I'm all done!

German word:	Sounds like...	It means...	German word:	Sounds like...	It means...
die Schultage	dee SHOOL-tah-guh	school days	*Mittwoch*	MIT-voke	Wednesday
die Schultasche	dee SHOOL-tash-uh	school bag	*Donnerstag*	DOH-ners-tahk	Thursday
Sonntag	SOHN-tahk	Sunday	*Freitag*	FRI-tahk	Friday
Montag	MOHN-tahk	Monday	*Samstag*	ZAMS-tahk	Saturday
Dienstag	DEENS-tahk	Tuesday			

On the first day of *Schule*,
The young children all own
A gift called a *Schultüte* —
A bright cardboard cone.

German word:	Sounds like. . .	And it means. . .
die Schule	dee SHOOL-uh	school
die Schultüte	dee SCHOOL-toot-uh	school cone

Die Schultüte is filled
With lots of sweet treats —
Gummibärchen, *Schokolade*,
And *Bonbons* to eat.

German word:	Sounds like. . .	And it means. . .
die Gummibärchen	dee gummy-BEAR-chen	gummy bears
die Schokolade	dee shaw-ko-LAH-duh	chocolate
die Bonbons	dee bohn-bohns	bonbons

$$1 + 2 + 3 + 4 = \underline{}$$

$$2 + 2 = \underline{}$$

My best subject is math,
So I don't have to fear
When teacher asks me to add
Eins, zwei, drei und vier.

German word:	Sounds like...	It means...	German word:	Sounds like...	It means...
Null	nul	zero	*vier*	feer	four
eins	eyns	one	*fünf*	foonf	five
zwei	tsvy	two	*sechs*	zeks	six
drei	dry	three			

Oops, my head's in a muddle.
Zwei und zwei isn't five!
When my addition's far off,
I feel like *ein Dummkopf.*

German word:	Sounds like...	It means...	German word:	Sounds like...	It means...
sieben	ZEE-ben	seven	*und*	unt	and
acht	akt	eight	*zwei und zwei*	tsvy unt tsvy	two plus two
neun	noyn	nine	*ein Dummkopf*	eyn DOOM-kof	a dummy
zehn	tsayn	ten			

German words can look *lang*.
They seem to weigh a ton.
But they're really like puzzles —
You combine words for fun.

German word:	Sounds like. . .	And it means. . .
lang	lahng	long
ein Zimmer	eyn TSIM-er	a room
das Bad	dahs bahd	bath
das Haus	dahs hows	the house
die Küche	dee KOO-chuh	the kitchen
das Eßzimmer	dahs ES-tsim-er	the dining room

Ein Zimmer is a room,
And bath is *ein Bad*.
So my bathwater simmers
In our *Badezimmer!*

German word:	Sounds like. . .	And it means. . .
das Wohnzimmer	dahs VOHN-tsim-er	the living room
die Garage	dee GAR-ahj-uh	the garage
das Badezimmer	dahs BAH-duh-tsim-er	the bathroom
das Schlafzimmer	dahs SHLAHF-tsim-er	the bedroom
das Kinderzimmer	dahs KIN-der-tsim-er	the children's room

After school I do homework,
So free time is rare.
But whenever I can,
I turn on *der Fernseher.*

German word:	Sounds like. . .	And it means. . .
der Fernseher	dayr FERN-zay-er	television set
die Mathematik	dee maht-uh-maht-eek	mathematics

Watch me play *Verstecken*.
I first count to ten —
Though peeking's *verboten*,
I cheat now and then.

German word:	Sounds like. . .	And it means. . .
Verstecken	fair-shteck-en	hide-and-seek
verboten	fair-boat-en	forbidden

To practice gymnastics,
I belong to a *Team.*
Watch me walk a straight line
At my club, *mein Verein.*

German word:	Sounds like. . .	And it means. . .
das Team	dahs teem	team
mein Verein	mine FAIR-ein	sports club

I really like *Fußball*.
When I kick the ball in,
My *Freunde* cheer loudly
'Cause we all like to win.

German word:	Sounds like. . .	And it means. . .
der Fußball	dayr FOOZ-bahl	soccer
meine Freunde	my-nuh FROYN-duh	friends

Shops close by six-thirty,
So when it's *fünf* on the clock,
I start to search for a gift
For my friend's *Geburtstag*.

German word:	Sounds like. . .	And it means. . .
fünf	foonf	five
der Geburtstag	dayr guh-BORTS-tahk	birthday

I look for *ein Spielzeug*,
Just right for that boy.
Perhaps a small *Zug*
Would be the right toy.

German word:	Sounds like. . .	And it means. . .
ein Spielzeug	eyn SHPEEL-zoyg	toy
der Zug	dayr sook	train
das Spielwarengeschäft	dahs SHPEEL-var-en-guh-sheft	toy store

He might like a toy *Pferd*.
I've been taught to be nice,
So I add *bitte*, of course,
When I ask, *"der Preis?"*

German word:	Sounds like. . .	And it means. . .
das Pferd	dahs faird	horse
bitte	bit-uh	please
der Preis?	dayr price	the price?

I pay with *Deutsche Mark*,
Plus a *Pfennig* or two.
The clerk hands me the horse,
And I say, *"Danke"* — "Thank you."

German word:	Sounds like. . .	And it means. . .
die Deutsche Mark	dee doych-uh mark	German money
der Pfennig	dayr FEN-ik	German coins
danke	DAHNK-eh	thank you

Going home I pass by
Our town's *Bäckerei*.
Fresh breads by the score
Fill the shelves of this store.

This *Brezel* is twisted
Just like a big bow.
It's salted and soft
Like a pillow of dough.

German word:	Sounds like. . .	And it means. . .
die Bäckerei	dee BEH-keh-rye	bakery
die Brezel	dee BRET-zel	pretzel
die Konditorei	dee kon-DEE-toh-rye	pastry shop
die Eisdiele	dee ICE-deel-uh	ice cream shop

Lunch is my main meal.
Dinner's small but complete.
Fleisch, *Sauerkraut* and a gravy
That tastes sour and sweet.

German word:	Sounds like. . .	And it means. . .
das Fleisch	dahs flysh	meat
das Sauerkraut	dahs SOUR-krowt	cabbage

Dessert's a rich pastry
With chocolate and cream.
Sehr gut! Very good!
I'd eat ten if I could!

German word:	Sounds like. . .	And it means. . .
Sehr gut!	zayr goot	very good!

I say, "*Ja*, I'd like more,"
But *meine Mutter* looks stern.
"You'd be sick in no time,
So the answer is *nein*."

German word:	Sounds like. . .	And it means. . .
Ja	yah	yes
meine Mutter	my-nuh MOO-ter	my mother
nein	nine	no

Within German borders,
Homes are neat
and well ordered.
So I clean up my room
And sweep *das Haus*
with a broom.

German word:	Sounds like. . .	And it means. . .
das Haus	dahs hows	house

It's German custom on Sundays
To enjoy peace and quiet.
So I find a small nook
Where *Ich lese ein Buch.*

German word:	Sounds like. . .	And it means. . .
Ich lese	eek lays-uh	I read
ein Buch	eyn boock	a book
die kleinen Mädchen	dee kly-nen MAYD-chen	the little girls

Holidays are special fun.
All Germans, big and small,
Wear strange and scary costumes
When we hold our *Karneval*.

German word:	Sounds like. . .	And it means. . .
der Karneval	dayr CAR-nuh-val	carnival

Ghosts, goblins and giants
Parade down *die Straße*.
"Omph pah pah" goes the band
In this fairytale land.

German word:	Sounds like. . .	And it means. . .
die Straße	dee STRAH-suh	the street

We can ride on *ein Boot*
Down our river, the Rhine.
The shore's lined with castles
From old German times.

German word:	Sounds like. . .	And it means. . .
ein Boot	eyn boat	boat

I hike paths through thick woods.
They're so *schwarz* with big trees
That it's named the Black Forest,
Or *Schwarzwald*, if you please.

German word:	Sounds like...	And it means...
schwarz	schvartz	black
der Schwarzwald	dayr SCHVARTZ-vald	Black Forest
der Campingplatz	dayr CAM-ping-plahtz	campground

In *Januar*, I ski all day.
The Alps are white with *Schnee*.
Or I hold tight with my mittens
And slide down on *mein Schlitten*.

German word:	Sounds like...	It means...	German word:	Sounds like...	It means...
der Schnee	dayr sh-nay	snow	*der Schlitten*	dayr sh-lit-en	sled
Januar	YA-noo-ar	January	*Juli*	YOO-lee	July
Februar	FAY-broo-ar	February	*August*	ow-GOOST	August
März	mayrtz	March	*September*	zep-TEM-ber	September
April	ah-PRIL	April	*Oktober*	ok-TOH-ber	October
Mai	my	May	*November*	noh-VEM-ber	November
Juni	YOO-nee	June	*Dezember*	dayts-EM-ber	December

If I lived in Germany
When night falls I'm all set,
'Cause it's cozy and warm
'Neath a thick *Federbett*.

The last words that I call
Are "*Gute Nacht*, one and all."

German word:	Sounds like. . .	And it means. . .
das Federbett	dahs FAY-der-bet	feather bed
gute Nacht	goo-tuh nahk-t	good night